Millions
and
Billions
and
Zillions
of
Ladybugs

Hope M. Jordan, Ph.D.

with Stu Morgan

Illustrated by: Kyra Moe

To order additional copies of this book, contact:
Xlibris
1-888-795-4274
www.Xlibris.com
Orders@Xlibris.com

Millions & Billions & Zillions of Ladybugs

Hope M. Jordan, Ph.D.

with Stu Morgan

Illustrated by: Kyra Moe

This story is dedicated to Arlene and Clay Morgan who were the inspiration for the grandparents in this story and to Rhiannon, Ricky, Joel, Nathan, Tyler, Mikaila, Logan, Morgan & Jordan (their grandchildren and great-grandchildren) as our models for Sam & Rion.

Samantha and Orion, Sam and Rion for short, will always remember the summer of their magical moon. It was a very special summer for three reasons. First, there was the magical moon. Second, they were spending the summer visiting their grandparents. And finally, there were the ladybugs. It certainly was an unforgettable summer!

Sam, who was six and half years' old and Rion, who was five lived in the city that summer. They liked living in the city, but when they got a chance to visit their grandparents far away in the country, they always had scads of fun. So, when their father told them that he and their mother had to travel during the summer while they visited their grandparents, they danced around him singing, "We get to visit grandma and grandpa!!! Hurray, we get to visit grandma and grandpa!!!"

Visiting grandma and grandpa was always fun because they did unusual things with their grandparents every single day. Sometimes it was walking in the woods to hunt for baby owls. Sometimes it was eating ice cream instead of a real lunch. Sometimes it was baking alphabet shaped pretzels or making Little Orphan Annie salads with pears and shaved carrots for hair. Sometimes it was roasting marshmallows over a campfire, and once they even grilled hotdogs outside in the middle of winter and ate them while wearing their mittens. Their grandparents played funny old songs on an old record player, danced in the living room, and told them stories about their dad when he was a boy. They never knew what surprises were waiting for them at grandma and grandpa's house, but they knew it would always be fun. However, the summer of the magical moon turned out to be the best summer ever, and maybe it was that very same moon that brought in the ladybugs. Who knows, when there is a magical moon, anything can happen.

They first noticed the moon the night their father brought them to their grandparent's house. Their father gazed up at the hazy sky and sighed, "Wow, I haven't seen a moon like that since I was a young man. That was the summer I met your mother." Rion asked his dad to tell them more about it, but dad didn't seem to hear him. He just had this weird smile on his face and a faraway look in his eyes as he gazed at the moon. A few minutes later he said, "That sure is a stunning moon." It was a marvelous moon. It was a full moon, but it seemed larger than usual, and it had an extraordinary, orange, misty glow. As it turned out, it was the very next day that their grandmother told them about the ladybugs, and that magical moon turned out to be the beginning of their adventure.

When they got up the next morning, grandma was busily washing the windows.

There were tiny highways of goopy yellow stuff on all the windows in the house. It seems that ladybugs leave a slimy trail behind as they travel across windows, so grandma was mumbling something as she scrubbed the windows.

She grumbled, "Where do they all come from? Do they blow in on the wind? Do they soar in with a falling star? Where do they all come from?"

"Where do all what come from?" questioned Sam.

"The darn ladybugs," sighed grandma grumpily as she scrubbed.

"Ladybugs are lucky, grandma. We should always take care of ladybugs. I just love ladybugs!!!" bubbled Sam. And it was true. Sam had shirts and shorts with ladybugs on them, socks with ladybugs on them; she even had a little purse with a ladybug on it, too.

"But there are millions and billions and zillions of them!!!" exclaimed her grandmother. Sam turned her head so grandma wouldn't see her giggle.

Just then Rion shuffled into the room. He was carrying his blanket and his ragged bear. His hair was a tasseled mess and he looked like he was barely awake. As he rubbed his sleepy eyes, he heard what grandma said and he asked, "Millions and billions and zillions of what, grandma?"

Grandma barked grumpily, "LADYBUGS, they are everywhere. Just wait, you'll see."

When the children went to the kitchen to have some oatmeal for breakfast, grandma asked them to open the window to let in some fresh air. As they pushed up the window, a pile of ladybugs tumbled onto the floor. The ladybugs scurried and flew in all directions as Sam and Rion squealed in delight, "Look grandma, millions and billions and zillions of ladybugs!!!" All the excitement woke Sassy, grandma's fluffy, old, black and white cat. He suddenly forgot his old age as he romped around the room trying to catch ladybugs, but it was no use. The ladybugs all got away. When grandpa came into the kitchen, the children could hardly wait to tell him about all the ladybugs.

Grandpa frowned and said, "I know. I just went downstairs to get my shirt out of the dryer, and when I turned on the basement light, guess what was piled on top of the clothes in the basket?"

"Millions and billions and zillions of ladybugs?" squealed the children in unison.

"Yes," replied grandpa. "I had to sweep them into the dustpan and take them outside."

"You didn't hurt them, did you?" questioned Sam with her hands on her hips and a scowl on her face.

"No, I didn't hurt them. I carried that basket full of ladybugs to the field out back and dumped them in the tall grass. But these ladybugs are becoming a problem. What will we do with millions and billions and zillions of ladybugs?"

Sam calmly smiled and sighed, "I don't think they are a problem at all." And with a faraway look in her eye she continued, "I bet they are here because of the magical moon."

Grandma and grandpa looked at one another as they had seen that faraway look before. They remembered the summer of the magical moon when their son, Sam and Rion's father, had met the love of his life. Grandpa and grandma exchanged a knowing smile, and grandpa replied, "You may just have a point there. The magical moon only appears once every ten years, and when it does, all kinds of seemingly impossible things can happen. I have heard tell that ladybugs are attracted to sweetness in people." He teasingly continued as he winked at grandma, "Maybe that is why your grandmother is surrounded by so many ladybugs!" As grandma blushed and gave grandpa a gentle shove, Sam just smiled and seemed to somehow understand.

A few weeks later, as their summer vacation in the country was coming to an end, Sam and Rion decided that they needed to go exploring in the fields and woods behind their grandparent's house. They knew that when they returned to the city they would not be able to romp after butterflies in grassy fields peppered with dandelions nearly as tall as they were. They would miss the stream full of minnows and the fluffy baby owls in the gigantic gnarly tree. They wanted to surprise their grandparents by bringing home a bucket of blackberries to put over ice cream for dinner. So, one warm afternoon while grandmother dozed in a lawn chair, they picked up the purple sand bucket, held their breath, and quietly tiptoed away from the farmhouse.

Once they were where grandma could no longer hear them, they gasped for air and began to giggle. They were on an adventure all by themselves. Grandma and grandpa had always insisted that the children never go off alone, but Sam and Rion felt they were grown up enough to hunt for some blackberries to surprise their grandparents. Off they went on their own.

They were only gone about twenty minutes when they found the blackberry patch and started to pick the plump, juicy, blackberries. Purple juice stained their hands and faces as they ate nearly as many as they put in the bucket. It only took a few minutes for the bucket to fill, so the carefree children turned to go home. As they turned, they were surprised to see a baby bear blocking their path. At first, they were startled and a little frightened, but the baby seemed to be friendly as it sat staring at their bulging bucket of wild blackberries. Rion decided that the baby bear looked hungry.

He said, "Sam, I think this baby is hungry. We have lots of blackberries. Let's share our blackberries with him."

Sam agreed, "You are right. He does look hungry, and he is very cute. We can pick more later for grandma and grandpa. Take the bucket over and let him have some berries."

Just as Rion was about to hold out his bucket to the baby bear, something rustled in the bushes next to the path. Adults know something about baby bears that Sam and Rion didn't know. This was one reason grandma and grandpa cautioned the children about going into the woods by themselves. Usually when you see a baby bear, there is a mother bear nearby. Suddenly, what seemed to the children like a ten-foot-tall mother bear stood up on her hind legs from behind some bushes and growled. Sam and Rion were shocked. They stood frozen on the path and could not think what to do.

Shortly after Sam and Rion had started down the path, grandma had woken up from her nap in the lawn chair. She saw that the children were not there, but she wasn't worried as she thought they were somewhere in the house with grandpa. When she went in the house to find the missing children, grandpa said he thought they were outside with her and he had not seen them. Both grandparents started to get nervous and went back outside to find the children. They looked under the apple trees, in the ditch filled with buttercups next to the road, in the garage, and then they asked the neighbors if they had seen their grandchildren. Nobody knew where the children were.

When the grandparents glanced toward the woods, they noticed that there was a huge cloud of ladybugs hovering near the path. As they walked toward the ladybugs, the cloud flew a little further ahead down the path. The ladybugs seemed to be guiding grandma and grandpa, so they followed the swarm into the woods. Suddenly, the ladybugs seemed to speed up, fly ahead, and hover over a spot further down the path.

The grandparents had just started walking toward the hovering ladybugs when they heard the deafening roar of a bear. Grandma let out a tiny squeal of fear as the blood drained from her face. Grandpa had heard that roar before in the woods. He did not panic, but he was very worried for the safety of his grandchildren. He bent down to pick up a large branch, told grandma to stay where she was as he quietly crept down the path.

As grandpa approached the spot where the children stood frozen in fear, he quickly assessed the situation. He knew that if anyone moved quickly or spoke loudly, they might startle the mother bear. The mother bear was only protecting her baby. If he could get the baby bear to move away from the children, he thought the mother bear might follow her baby. This would give the children time to get away from the bears to safety.

The children were so frightened that they had not noticed the cloud of ladybugs hovering over their heads. They did not even notice grandpa quietly standing on the path behind the bears. When grandma came up behind grandpa with a bowl of honey, the children finally started paying attention to what was going on. Grandpa was used to grandma thinking for herself, so it did not surprise him that she had a plan of her own to help get those bears' attention. As everyone knows, bears love honey. Grandpa took the bowl of honey she held out to him and quietly tried to get the baby bear to look at him.

The baby started to wiggle his nose as he began to smell the honey and started walking toward the bowl that grandpa held out. The mother bear was carefully watching her baby the whole time. Grandpa gingerly walked off the path, staying just ahead of the baby, while the mother bear followed behind. He led the baby to a creek that was a few hundred feet away from the path.

As soon as the bears were away from the path, grandma motioned the children to be quiet, but to come to her. The children followed her silent directions, but they kept watching grandpa and the bears. Now that the mother bear was rambling away from them, they were nervous about grandpa's safety. The children slowly worked their way toward grandma as she knelt to gather them in a silent, relieved, hug.

Grandpa could see that the children were no longer in danger, but he knew that he was still in peril. He kept slowly leading the bears toward the creek. When he got to the edge of the creek, he carefully set the bowl of honey on the ground and crossed the creek walking away from the bears. The baby bear tumbled toward the honey with the mother bear right behind. As grandpa, slowly and quietly headed toward home, the baby bear nearly stuck her whole head in the bowl of honey and began contentedly lapping it up. The mother bear sat watching her baby and hardly seemed to notice grandpa sneaking away.

When grandpa arrived home safely, he again saw the cloud of ladybugs hovering near the apple trees. They seemed to be protectively watching over the children as grandma scolded them for going into the woods alone. She reminded them how dangerous that was and how they had worried their grandparents. She was getting ready to remind them that grandpa might still be in danger. When she looked up and saw grandpa, a small tear of relief rolled down her cheek. Her whole family was home safe and she squeezed them together in a great big hug. She was so happy that everyone was home and safe at last. Suddenly, the children noticed the swarm of ladybugs!

Sam cried out, "Look, there are millions and billions and zillions of ladybugs!

Rion replied, "I think there are gadwillions of ladybugs!" His response struck everyone as terribly silly and they all started to laugh.

Grandpa explained, "The ladybugs helped us find you. They showed us where you were on the path, and they stayed with you to keep you safe until we arrived."

Sam smiled and simply replied, "I just love ladybugs."

This time Rion agreed, "Me, too."

Even though the ladybugs had sometimes been a bother this summer, their grandparents felt the same way.

A few days later when their parents came to take them home, their father did not seem surprised by their adventure. When they told him, he simply pulled their mother closer to his side and declared, "You never know what might happen in the summer of the magical moon!" Their mother smiled backed and seemed to understand. The children never forgot the summer of the magical moon, the baby bear, or the millions and billions and zillions of ladybugs.

Topics for Further Investigation, Thought & Discussion

(There are several suggested links below. Sometimes web addresses for links are updated. If you do not find the information at these links, please do an online search for updated sites using key words.)

Moon

Is the moon magical? Some people think so. What do you think? You may want to do a further investigation of the moon and there are some suggestions for sites you might want to study listed below. Or – maybe you want to write a song about the moon, paint a beautiful picture, or do a video science report!

The Moon Facts About the Moon for Kids

http://www.planetsforkids.org/moon-moon.html

The Moon Cool Moon Facts for Kids

http://www.coolkidfacts.com/moon-facts-for-kids/

Neil Armstrong Biography at Ducksters.com

http://www.ducksters.com/biography/explorers/neil_armstrong.php

The Moon for Kids Educational Video (4 min. video)

https://www.youtube.com/watch?v=B-b4XvuQo1Y

Ladybugs

Some of what is included in our story regarding ladybugs is real and some is not. Can you do an investigation to find out more about ladybug facts? Do ladybugs leave "highways of goopy yellow stuff?" Are ladybugs bugs? Do ladybugs swarm and if so, why? What do ladybugs eat? Can you think of other ladybug questions you would like to answer? Maybe you want to write a poem about ladybugs, draw a beautiful picture or design a t-shirt with fabric paint!

National Geographic (great ladybug facts) http://animals.nationalgeographic.com/animals/bugs/ladybug/

National Geographic for Kids (kid friendly ladybug facts)

http://kids.nationalgeographic.com/animals/ladybug/#ladybug-map.jpg

10 Fascinating Facts About Ladybugs

https://www.thoughtco.com/
fascinating-facts-about-ladybugs-1968120

What Do Ladybugs Eat: Facts about Ladybugs (5 min video)

https://www.youtube.com/watch?v=e-FCVIdDhQI

Bears

Do bears eat honey & blackberries? Are mother bears protective of their cubs? Have you ever visited a zoo to see the bears? What kind of bears did the children in this story most likely see? If you visit the zoo, maybe you want to take some pictures of the bears! Maybe you want to write a report about bears or design a crossword puzzle to share with your family or teacher. Following are some sites you might like to investigate.

Brown Bears National Geographic for Kids

http://kids.nationalgeographic.com/animals/
brown-bear/#brown-bear-fish-stream.jpg

Bear Facts Index

http://www.kidzone.ws/lw/bears/facts.htm

American Black Bear

http://naturemappingfoundation.org/natmap/
facts/american_black_bear_k6.html

Disney Nature Bears (2min. video)

https://www.youtube.com/watch?v=DAO0e9_L_ss

Printed in the United States
By Bookmasters